The Adventures
of Gusto the Dragon

The Rise of
The Grand Protector

CU00823161

Welcome to the magical world of
Gusto the Dragon.

Books in the series of
The Adventures of Gusto The Dragon

Book 1

The Rise of the Grand Protector

Book 2

The Secret Islands of the Seven Clouds

Book 3

Challenge of Destiny

Let Gusto be your hero!

The Adventures
of Gusto the Dragon

The Rise of
The Grand Protector

KATHLEEN GARDINER

First published 2007
by Nutritional Wisdom Publishing
www.gustothedragon.com

All rights reserved

No part of this publication may be reproduced
or transmitted in any form or by any means,
electronic, mechanical, photocopying, recording,
or by any information storage or retrieval system,
without the prior permission of the publisher.

Copyright © 2007 Kathleen Gardiner
Illustrations & Cover illustrations
copyright © 2007 Kathleen Gardiner.

Illustrations by Neville Swaine.

The moral right of the author has been asserted.

A CIP catalogue record of this book is
available from the British Library.

ISBN 978-0-9557357-0-7

Typeset by Croft Publications
The Croft, 8 St James Meadow, Boroughbridge YO51 9NW

Printed and bound by
Smith Settle Printers & Bookbinders Ltd.
Gateway Drive, Yeadon LS19 7XY

CONTENTS

PART 1
The Tomboy Princess & The Giant Dragon

PART 2
Gusto at the Inside-Outside Garden Party

PART 3
Gusto in the Domain of the Dragons

Note to parents from the author

***

The Adventures
of
Gusto the Dragon

This series has brought together my passion
for nutrition and writing.
Each book embraces strong messages
of nutrition and friendship.
Books 2 & 3 also include other ethical issues.

I hope you and your children will enjoy the web of
magic, mystery and adventure that flows
through the series.

Thank you for purchasing
The Adventures of Gusto the Dragon.
May Gusto become your hero too!

You can find out more about the series by visiting
www.gustothedragon.com, where you can learn
about the books and meet the main characters.
Purchasing information is also provided.

ACKNOWLEDGEMENTS

I would like to thank Leila, Malcolm and Linda
for their support, encouragement
and friendship.

For Butter Bean & Sweet Pea

Part 1

The Tomboy Princess
&
The Giant Dragon

Chapter 1

Princess Peaches

v

Sid Chucklecheeks

Princess Peaches is a wise, kind and caring fairy princess. She lives in the Kingdom of Wisdom, high in the Magic Mountains with her parents King Manuka and Queen Honey.

Peaches is a tomboy, who loves nothing more than going down to the meadow to play with her favourite brightly coloured ball and to meet up with her meadow friends. She always wears a lilac track suit with 'PP' in big silver letters on the back, lilac cap and red trainers.

Peaches goes everywhere in her trainers. She thinks they are really cool.

Every day her friend Silence, the Mountain Eagle, takes Peaches to the meadow and then brings her safely home. She sits behind his head and holds on to his strong feathers. He has a beautiful bright blue feather in the centre of his forehead unlike the other eagles, which makes him easy to recognise. Peaches tucks her long, black, curly locks into her lilac peaked-cap, before Silence effortlessly swoops down the mountains to the meadow below, where Peaches meets many of her friends. All the meadow and woodland creatures know and love Princess Peaches

The meadow is full of pretty wild flowers such as daisies, buttercups, clover, poppies and cowslips. It is overlooked by the Magic Mountains, which protect all in their view including the meadow.

One of Peaches' favourite meadow playmates is Sid Chucklecheeks, the spider. She often practises scoring goals in a net made from a double layer of Sid's carefully woven webs. The webs are held in place by four twigs from a nearby apple tree. Sid acts as goal keeper and scores a point for every goal he saves. After all, he has eight legs, which should make it quite a challenge for the fairy princess! However, Sid is

a bit slow and has a strange sense of humour which gives Peaches an enormous advantage.

Peaches always screams with delight, "Goal, goal, another point for me!" every time she scores a goal, and her wings start to flutter uncontrollably as they always do whenever she is excited. Sid chuckles so much at Peaches' reaction that he finds it difficult to concentrate. Before he has a chance to recover, Peaches scores more goals.

Peaches knows that the louder she shrieks in delight every time she scores, the more Sid shakes uncontrollably with laughter. However, there comes a point when Peaches cannot play because she is laughing so much at Sid, by which time all the creatures in the meadow watching the spectacle start rolling

around in hoots of infectious laughter too.

Chapter 2

Peaches meets
Gusto the Giant Dragon

One day Princess Peaches was playing with her ball in the meadow when she heard the sound of crying coming from Bluebell Wood just across the meadow. Being a curious fairy, she took flight as fast as her fairy wings could carry her towards the wood. She wanted to find out who could be crying, and why?

The woods were covered in a carpet of bluebells and the trees were host to many beautiful songbirds and other woodland creatures. They always became excited when they saw Princess Peaches. The birds sang louder and you could hear the scampering sounds of the squirrels and rabbits as they appeared, as if from nowhere, to greet their fairy friend. This time though, Peaches was in a hurry and didn't have time to stop and play.

The sobbing grew louder and louder as she went deeper into the wood. The sun was shining brightly through the trees, lighting up the way to where the noise was coming from. It had become almost deafening when Peaches spotted an enormous fat dragon lying under a magnificent oak tree, crying his heart out. His giant tears had created a big pool of water around him. Sunlight flickered through the trees onto the pool of tears, making it look like a mass of shimmering diamonds dancing around the distressed giant dragon.

At first Princess Peaches was a little scared, which was unusual for her because she wasn't afraid of anything. Her loving nature made her feel sorry for this poor creature and she wanted to help him.

Without giving it another thought, and in spite of her slight nervousness, Princess Peaches slowly flew down to the edge of the pool of tears in full view of the dragon.

"Don't cry Mr. Dragon, nothing is worth so many tears. Why are you so sad?" asked Princess Peaches, in a soft, gentle voice.

The troubled dragon wiped his eyes with his powerful right paw to see more clearly where the unfamiliar, yet soothing voice came from. When the dragon managed to focus his tear filled eyes on the fairy princess, he was startled and embarrassed. In a shaky voice, and still crying, the dragon managed to ask,

"Wh…wh…who…are you...:and why should you … care about me?"

"Why shouldn't I care about you? I don't like people, fairies or dragons to be sad. Tell me what is so bad that you are crying like this. I might be able to help you," replied Princess Peaches.

"You … don't look … like a princess. If you were a princess you wouldn't have a dirty track suit on …. and mud on your face", said the dragon, who was still crying.

"I *am* a princess," said Peaches, in a dignified way, slightly taken aback at the giant dragon questioning her honesty. "My name is Princess Peaches and I come from the Kingdom of Wisdom high in the Magic Mountains. I heard you crying when I was playing with my ball in the meadow beyond the wood. Please tell me why you are so sad? You can trust me; I really would like to help you."

"Well, I cannot play boys games with my friends anymore or blow fire from my big nostrils. I just don't have the energy you see," wailed the pitiful creature, "and what's more, I'm very hungry and I don't feel well."

"Oh dear," said Peaches, "No wonder you are so miserable and unhappy, but I know just how I can help you." Immediately, the dragon stopped crying and sat up in his pool of tears, not able to take his huge, sorrowful eyes off the little fairy.

"You can?" replied the dragon in a croaky questioning voice. "Are you sure? After all you are so tiny; how on earth can you help me?"

"First of all it would be nice to know your name," said Peaches, feeling pleased that at last she had the creature's attention. "You can call me Peaches, there's no need to address me as Princess, *even though I am a real princess*," she announced, in a slightly raised voice.

"Oh…er, thank you.. er, Peaches," replied Gusto, slightly over-awed and bewildered by his new friend. "My name is Gusto. I was named Gusto because I used to be able to shoot big gusts of fire from my nostrils, much further than any of my friends in the Domain of the Dragons. I used to get such a thrill, none of my friends could beat me and now, all I can muster is a little puff of smoke!"

"Well, hello Gusto, I am very pleased to meet you. I may have the answer to all your problems but, it won't be easy. You must do everything I tell you," said Peaches, in a firm but reassuring way.

Gusto could not believe his ears. "I will do anything to be a strong and healthy dragon again," he responded, as he looked at Peaches in amazement.

"I have noticed all sorts of empty packets floating around you on your pool of tears," said Peaches, in a questioning tone, and knowing full well what they had previously contained. "Can you tell me what was in them?"

"Oh!" replied Gusto, with a guilty look on his face. "They contained my lunch….. and my dinner."

"Yes but what was in the packets Gusto? What did you eat for your lunch and dinner – and in-between?" questioned Peaches.

Gusto looked bashful and slowly replied in a voice as low as a dragon can go, "Crisps,….

sweets, …….. biscuits, …….. chocolate cake and sandwiches …….. with lots of butter and jam."

Peaches flew up and sat on the end of Gusto's wide nostrils and gave him a gentle reassuring pat on the side of his long, knobbly dragon jaw. "You are such a handsome dragon Gusto and I am very pleased you are my friend," said Peaches, who really wanted to comfort Gusto, because she knew he was feeling bad about himself.

"The problem is, you really are eating too much unhealthy food. You will never have lots of energy to shoot fire from your nostrils, or play boys games if you continue eating so much of this kind of food. It is making you feel ill, tired and unhappy, and causing you to put on so much extra weight," said Peaches.

Peaches pulled out her wand, which had been tightly tucked into her belt, and waved it three times around the pool of tears surrounding her and Gusto. To Gusto's complete surprise, the pool disappeared along with all the rubbish left behind from his 'so-called' meals, and the dancing diamonds were replaced by a host of giant-sized shiny, colourful fruits. These included lots of berries, apples, oranges, bananas, pineapples, pears, mangoes and the most beautiful peaches he had ever seen.

"From now on Gusto, every time you want to eat sweets, crisps, biscuits or cakes, eat a piece of fruit instead." Before Peaches could say anything else, Gusto had picked up a large juicy peach. The juice was flowing down his cheeks as he relished the delicious soft fruit – he was in heaven! To avoid getting swamped in the juice Peaches flew onto a low hanging branch of the nearby oak tree.

Gusto's eyes widened. He could not believe what was happening and a huge smile of satisfaction appeared on his amazing dragon face. "That was so good Peaches, please may I have another one?" asked Gusto.

"Of course you can," said Peaches, giggling at the new found pleasure the fruit had given this wonderful dragon. "Why don't you try an apple this time?" With that, all Peaches

could hear was the crunch, crunch, crunch of Gusto munching his way through a big, shiny, red apple; she found the noise was almost deafening.

"Of course, as well as the fruit, it is very important that you eat vegetables every day. *Fruits and vegetables are full of magic powers, which fight off nasty infections and diseases* and make you feel so much better," said Peaches.

Gusto nodded as he continued to enjoy the fruits and found he was particularly partial to strawberries, blackberries and raspberries. As he licked his lips he was careful not to knock Peaches off her perch with his long, forked, dragon tongue.

"Would you like to come and play ball with me now in the meadow?" asked Peaches. "It will be fun and good exercise."

Gusto gave a loud burp and, after apologising, and looking very embarrassed, replied in an excited voice, "Oooh, yes please Peaches, it's ages since someone asked me to play with them. You really are my very best friend."

Peaches smiled to herself as Gusto got clumsily to his feet. She fluttered her delicate wings and took flight, leading the way through the woods. Gusto waddled behind in hot pursuit, excited at the invitation to play ball in the meadow with his new friend.

Chapter 3
Another treat for Gusto

After enjoying a fun time in the meadow together, the two friends made their way back to the old oak tree in the woods. Peaches had promised Gusto a final treat before having to fly back to the Kingdom of Wisdom in the Magic Mountains.

The two new friends sat down beneath the spreading branches of the majestic oak tree, on a carpet of speckled sunshine and cool shade. Peaches pulled out her magic wand again and this time provided a feast which included lots of fresh fish, delicious vegetables and large platters of beautiful, colourful salads, lean juicy steaks and a bowl of long, curly strips of hot pasta.

She knew that dragons had enormous appetites and could eat enough food in one meal to feed the whole fairy population in the Kingdom of Wisdom.

Peaches told Gusto that this type of food would keep him happy, healthy and full of energy and the magic powers they contained would help him live a longer life.

"You must get lots of exercise as well, every day if you can. You will soon be able to blow lots of fire from your nostrils and have many new dragon friends," assured Peaches.

The smell of the special picnic floated through the forest under the noses of all the woodland creatures. Before long, they were all tucking into the forest feast.

All Peaches meadow and forest friends were there, including Sid the chuckling spider. They laughed so much that Gusto forgot all his problems. He really enjoyed his healthy meal and the company of his new found friends.

Chapter 4
The Folk of the Enchanted Wood!

They had just about finished their woodland feast when Scamp, the squirrel, came running through the woods towards Peaches. Almost out of breath Scamp said to Peaches, "There are three human children in the wood. They have been picking bluebells and have suddenly realised they are lost. I think they may need your help Peaches."

Peaches told Gusto that she would return as soon as possible.

"Lead the way Scamp!" said Peaches.

It didn't take long before Peaches noticed the three children sitting in a small clearing in the wood, two girls and a boy. The oldest girl was trying to reassure the other two children that they would soon find their way out of the wood and that there was nothing to worry about. Peaches suspected that she was quite worried too and was just doing her best to comfort the other two children.

Peaches told Scamp to wait behind a tree whilst she approached the children. She flew onto a nearby branch of a sycamore tree within a short distance of the children.

"Excuse me," said Peaches, hoping not to startle the children. "My name is Peaches and I was just wondering if I could help you? I overheard you saying you may be lost."

The children couldn't believe their eyes — a real live fairy was actually speaking to them! The eldest child eventually said, "My name is Alice, and this is my brother Joseph and my younger sister Sophie. We were picking bluebells for our mother when suddenly, we realised we were lost. In fact, we don't really know how we got here in the first place. All I can remember is reading a story to Sophie and Joseph at bed time, and then, the next moment, here we all are! Can you help us?" asked Alice, who was bewildered at not being able to understand the situation.

"I'm sure I can help you Alice," replied Peaches. "There is no need to worry any more but, before I take you home, would you like to meet a very friendly dragon and some of the woodland creatures?"

Joseph's eyes nearly popped out of his head, "Are you serious Peaches, can we really meet a live dragon?"

"I am very serious Joseph, in fact, he is very close to where we are standing now and I know he would love to say 'hello' to you all. Follow me and no harm will come to you."

The children followed Peaches, full of excitement, all clutching a bunch of freshly picked bluebells. Alice held Sophie's hand, while Joseph went ahead of them. "This is a once in a lifetime moment you can only *dream* about," thought Joseph.

Peaches approached Gusto with a twinkle in her eyes. "Gusto, I would like you to meet Alice, Joseph and Sophie. They were lost in the wood but wanted to meet you before they go home," said Peaches.

"It is an honour to meet you all. I have met so many new friends today, I can't believe how lucky I am," said Gusto.

"You can talk as well Gusto," said Joseph. "WOW! Wait until I tell my friends at school that I have *talked* to a real dragon. We are the lucky ones. Can you fly, and how far can you blow fire out of your nostrils?" continued

Joseph, hardly coming up for air he was so excited.

Gusto replied, "Well, you see Joseph, at the moment, I cannot blow fire from my nostrils, only a small puff of smoke, as I am not very healthy or fit, all because of the unhealthy food I have been eating (Gusto then demonstrated the puff of smoke which actually created quite a cloud over everyone) but, Peaches is going to help me."

"From now on I am going to eat up all my vegetables and eat fruit between meals instead of sugary and fatty snacks. I am also going to start doing lots of exercise, until I am fit and healthy again. Then, I will be able to blow lots of fire from my nostrils," continued Gusto.

"I think you are great Gusto," said Joseph. "Can we come and see you again when you can blow fire from your nostrils?"

"I hope that we can all get together again soon, Joseph. I would really like that," replied Gusto.

Alice and Sophie had been making friends with all the other woodland creatures. Sophie liked the baby rabbits and the cheeky squirrels. Alice had a chat with Oswald, the wise owl and Shandy, the roe deer. The three children felt as if they were in wonderland.

"I'm afraid it's time for you all to go home now," said Peaches. "I'm sure your mother will be wondering where you have got to." Peaches was also concerned that her own parents might be worried, as she had been away from home longer than usual and she knew that Silence would be waiting for her.

The children all said their 'goodbyes' to Gusto and the woodland creatures, before following Peaches back to the clearing in the wood.

"It's been such fun being with you all, but it's now time for me to help you find your way home," said Peaches to the three children.

"I am going to point my wand towards the sky and I want you all to look up and watch it very carefully; do not take your eyes off the twinkling wand." The children were mesmerised, as they fixed their eyes on Peaches wand and one by one they fell asleep.

The children were woken by the sound of their mother's voice softly saying, "What are you all doing on the floor in Sophie's bedroom, and where did you find these lovely bunches of bluebells?"

Their mother and father gently lifted them into their own beds. The children were exhausted and fell straight back to sleep the minute their heads touched their pillows.

The following morning the children were beside themselves, every one of them speaking at the same time trying to tell their parents their own version of what had happened the night before. Their parents listened to them but, they were not able to make any sense of their story. However, the children were very persistent in telling them what had happened.

The strangest thing was not being able to account for the bunches of beautiful bluebells which each one of the children had been clutching when their mother found them in Sophie's bedroom. "After all, it is summer and there are no bluebells in flower at this time of year," thought the children's mother, feeling confused about the whole scenario. "It really is a mystery," she whispered under her breath.

After the children had gone to school, the children's mother went into Sophie's bedroom. She picked the book up from the floor which Alice had been reading to her brother and sister the previous evening. It was called, The Folk of The Enchanted Wood!

"Where did those bluebells come from?" she thought, shaking her head.

Chapter 5
Time to go home

Before leaving, Peaches asked Gusto if he would like to come to her birthday party in a few weeks time. His eyes lit up and without hesitation he said he would be thrilled to go to the party. It was to be a party full of special surprises.

Peaches was sad to say 'goodbye' to Gusto. She knew she had met a very special friend but, she knew that Silence would be waiting for her in the meadow. It was time to go home.

As usual, Peaches faithful friend, Silence, was there in the meadow. She flew onto his back and gave him a big hug. She loved Silence and always appreciated him for taking her, every day, to the meadow and returning her safely to the Kingdom of Wisdom at the end of the day.

As they flew up between the Magic Mountains, Peaches couldn't help thinking how lucky she was to have so many wonderful friends.

The giant dragon and the fairy princess became the very best of friends and often met beneath the oak tree for a delicious healthy picnic, after playing together in the meadow.

Custo kept his promise not to eat lots of unhealthy food and he eventually became the finest dragon in the whole Domain of the Dragons. He was soon able to blow lots of fire from his nostrils.

All the dragons loved him and wanted to be his friend, although his best friend remained the tomboy fairy, Princess Peaches.

Part 2

Gusto at the
Inside-Outside Garden Party

Chapter 6

Party Time

Princess Peaches is a very special fairy. All the fairies in the Kingdom of Wisdom are very wise but Princess Peaches is the wisest fairy of them all, apart from her parents, King Manuka and Queen Honey and, of course, her great uncle Erudite, the Wise Wizard.

It was Peaches birthday and her parents had organised a special party for her. Everyone in the Kingdom of Wisdom was invited. Peaches loved dancing and her favourite band, The Birds & Bees, was booked to play. They are 'ace'! Peaches couldn't wait for the party to start.

Peaches asked her mother if she could invite her friend Gusto, the giant dragon, whom she had met a few weeks ago in Bluebell Wood. Her mother agreed but, because Gusto was so big, the party had to be held in their Inside-Outside Garden, which is situated right in the middle of their 'larger than life' crystal Palace. The garden is in this particular place so that it can be viewed from any part of the Palace.

Peaches told all her friends that she was inviting a surprise guest who lived many mountains away.

The Inside-Outside Garden is enormous, with all kinds of trees and plants, waterfalls, fountains and fish ponds and most important of all, their prized vegetable plots and fruit orchards. The folk of the Kingdom of Wisdom ate these favourite foods every day to help them keep healthy and wise.

The clock struck six o'clock and the guests started to arrive, each one bringing Peaches a lovely present.

Peaches' friend, Anastasia-Florence, called 'Flo' for short, brought Peaches a magic pair of red trainers. She knew that red is Peaches' favourite colour. A note inside the box said, *'Put me back in my box every time you take me off, and the next time you open the box I will be clean and just like new'*.

"Wow!" said Peaches, as she kicked off her trainers and put her new magic ones on,

"This will save me cleaning my trainers every evening when I return from the meadow; they get so dirty by the end of the day! Thank you so much Flo, this is a super present."

Taliya Grace, Peaches' cousin, gave Peaches a new red rucksack with silver straps. It had a special compartment for her freshly squeezed orange juice and a net for her ball, which was attached across the base of the rucksack, like a hammock.

"If you ever get hungry Peaches," said Taliya Grace, "close your eyes and wish for your favourite treat. Then open up the special flap at the front of the rucksack and your wish will be granted."

"Oh!" exclaimed Peaches, "that means I will be able to have a chicken and avocado sandwich and a dish of my favourite berry crumble whenever I feel hungry. Thank you so much Taliya, my mouth is watering already," said Peaches.

Sid Chucklecheeks, the spider, came running across the lawn towards Peaches to wish her a 'Happy Birthday' and frightened lots of the fairies! "Don't worry," assured Peaches, "Sid is a good playmate. We play football together in the meadow and he is great fun. Come over and meet him."

The fairies slowly plucked up enough courage to come over to say 'hello' to Sid.

"It's a pleasure to meet you all. Why don't you come and join us in the meadow? We could have a super game of football if you all joined in," said Sid, trying to put the fairies at ease.

Peaches screeched "Oh! That's a great idea Sid". Sid started to chuckle as he always does whenever Peaches gets excited. The trouble is, whenever Sid starts to chuckle he has trouble stopping and then his whole body shakes with laughter. This makes Peaches laugh and before long, as usual, everyone is laughing at the chuckling spider.

The sun had gone down but it was a warm and calm evening. The Inside-Outside Garden looked beautiful, it was lit by fairy lights, flickering candles and colourful lanterns. Red balloons were suspended in the trees. Indeed it was a magical sight.

Peaches was so excited her wings would not stop fluttering as she anticipated Gusto's arrival. She was looking forward to introducing him to the entire fairy kingdom.

Chapter 7
WOW! What an entrance!

Peaches didn't have to wait long. She looked up
into the starlit sky and saw Gusto circling high
above the garden. He had flown many miles
from the Domain of the Dragons beyond the
Secret Islands of the Seven Clouds to be with
her on this special occasion. In great excitement
Gusto released an enormous gust of bright
orange flames from his giant nostrils to let
Peaches know it was him. She clapped her
hands as her friend showed off his star act.
All the guests screamed with shock at the
unfamiliar monster in the sky, but any fears

were lost when they realised that this was the surprise guest they were all looking forward to meeting, and WOW! - What an entrance!

Gusto very carefully started his descent, arriving perfectly in the centre of the grand lawn. Peaches quickly flew over to meet him, landing on the top of Gusto's head, before sliding down his long forehead between his large eyes, just managing to stop in the middle of his dragon snout. She couldn't sit in her favourite spot at the end of Gusto's nostrils because they were too warm from his dramatic fire-blasting display

"Oh Gusto, you made it. You must come and say 'hello' to all my friends," said Peaches, who looked stunning in her new pink party dress

which sparkled like the stars and of course, her new pair of magic trainers.

Gradually, all the guests from the fairy kingdom surrounded the gentle giant. They all fell in love with him, just as Peaches had. Gusto wallowed in their warm welcome.

The King and Queen brought Gusto a platter of his favourite giant juicy peaches to refresh him from his journey and said how delighted they were that he was able to join them on this special occasion. Gusto blushed slightly at meeting the King and Queen and at the kindness they bestowed upon him.

Everyone helped themselves to the magnificent, healthy birthday feast prepared by the royal caterers.

In the centre of the table was a beautiful, fruit birthday cake. The top layer was in the shape of a giant peach with 'PP' lit up in the centre of a big twinkling star. The second layer was completely covered in red berries and the bottom layer was decorated with cherries, black grapes, apricots and thin slices of red water melon.

After a long relaxing meal, The Birds & Bees turned up the tempo of the music. Gusto waved his head from side to side to the beat, while everyone else danced in a large fairy circle around him. Sid Chucklecheeks joined in and showed off with his dancing. He got carried away so much that his eight legs became all tangled up and he had to roll on his back to

unravel them. This caused hysterics with Peaches and her friends. Their tummies ached with laughter.

Whenever Sid is around you can guarantee that everyone will end up in stitches!

Chapter 8
The Magic Strawberries

In spite of eating the delicious party food, all the
fairies helped themselves to berry fruits from
the fruit garden during the course of the
evening, dancing all the while in between the
bushes and trees. Each fairy picked a berry for
Gusto until there were enough for him to enjoy
with a good dollop of fresh vanilla yogurt. There
were strawberries, raspberries, blackberries and
blueberries, all Gusto's favourite berries. *The*

fairies loved fruits; they knew they had magic powers to help fight off nasty infections and diseases.

Hidden between the fruit trees were tiny, pink 'surprise' boxes, wrapped in golden silk thread woven especially by Peaches' friends, the silk worms, who lived at the bottom of the garden.

Surprises were never sweets because the wise fairies didn't like sweet sugary things.

Each little box contained a special magic strawberry. It was special because a wish would be granted with the first bite of the fruit, so each fairy had to think very carefully before taking the first bite of this special strawberry.

Taliya Grace closed her eyes and wished for a ball so that she could practise playing football before going to the meadow with Sid and Peaches. When she opened her eyes, there was a bright, shiny, purple ball with 'TG' written across it in bright pink letters. She danced up and down and twirled around and around with joy. It was just what she wanted.

Anastasia-Florence wished for a microphone so that she could sing 'Happy Birthday' with The Birds & Bees band. She loved singing and thought this would be a nice surprise for Peaches. When she opened her eyes there was a shining silver microphone that didn't need any wires or plugs. She could use it anywhere she liked. "Oh, thank you magic strawberry!" said Flo, as she, too, danced about with joy. She couldn't wait to hatch her plan to sing with The Birds & Bees.

It was Sid's turn. He quickly opened the delicate pink box and carefully took out the red strawberry. He looked over at Peaches with a mischievous look upon his face, and then closed his eyes and took a bite of the big red fruit.

His wish was to *just once*, beat his friend at point scoring when she tried to kick her ball into the net, that he was supposed to guard as goal keeper.

"Well," said Peaches, "what did you wish for? Nothing has appeared!"

"You will soon find out," said Sid, as he fell about laughing at the look on Peaches' face. "Tomorrow, all will be revealed."

Peaches knew Sid was up to something but didn't have a clue what it could be. She would have to wait until they met the following day in the meadow to find out.

There was even a surprise for Gusto, given to him by Peaches so that he wouldn't be left out. It was a magic peach tree for him to plant in his own garden in the Domain of the Dragons. The label said, *'Whenever you pick a peach from my branches another one will appear'*. You can imagine Gusto's delight at receiving such a special present. Not only would he enjoy the fruits of this magic peach tree, but it would always remind him of this very special, perfect evening.

Chapter 9
The Wise Wizard's Surprise

At nine o'clock, there was a fanfare of trumpets. The finale was about to begin. The lead singer of The Birds & Bees requested the attention of everyone before introducing Flo. She looked so pretty in her pale blue party dress. Flo stepped forward with her new microphone and the band started to play as she sang 'Happy Birthday' to Peaches. When she had finished, everybody at the party sang it all over again.

Peaches was so happy! She flew over to Flo and gave her a big hug. "Thank you so much Flo, that was such a lovely surprise! I didn't know you could sing," said Peaches. "Now

you have your new microphone you will be able to sing with The Birds & Bees at all their performances. They have been looking for another singer to complete their band."

Suddenly, all the lights went out and everyone went silent. A star seemed to fall from the sky, heading for the lawn right in front of Peaches. It burst into hundreds of little stars as it appeared to hit the ground. In the circle of light, her favourite Uncle Erudite appeared, the Wise Wizard of the Magic Mountains.

The candles in the garden began to flicker again and the fairy lights once again started to twinkle. The Wise Wizard pointed his wand towards a large box which had appeared out of thin air between him and Peaches. He asked Peaches to count slowly to three. "One….. two….. three," counted Peaches. The box fell apart and the most beautiful, fluffy, white puppy came running towards her. It had two large black eyes and an even bigger black nose. He stopped, as if by magic, right in front of her. She thought he was going to knock her over.

"Let me introduce you to Precious," said the Wise Wizard to Peaches. "He is a very special puppy and will protect you wherever you are. He has unique powers which you will discover as things happen over time." Precious lifted up his front paw, as if to invite his new owner to shake hands, which she instinctively did. They looked into each others' eyes and a

special bond was made. It was as if they had known each other forever.

Gusto wasn't quite sure about Peaches' new friend and started to feel a bit left out but, Peaches immediately took Precious over to meet him and said to Precious, "This is Gusto, my special friend. I want you to protect and love him, just as much as you do me. We can all play together in the meadow." This made Gusto feel very special and happy.

Before leaving Gusto said he had a birthday present for Peaches. It was an invitation to see him compete in the dragon games in the Domain of the Dragons, the very best seats of course, in the Giant Dragon Arena. However, there was something missing from the invitation.

"Your name is the only one on the invitation Peaches," said Gusto. "I would be very honoured if our new friend Precious would join you."

"Oh Gusto, this is the best present you could have given me! Thank you so much! Now I have something else exciting to look forward to." Precious wagged his tale in sheer delight and let out a series of puppy yelps.

Before Gusto left, Peaches gave him a big chunk of her birthday cake to eat on his long journey home and a bag of his favourite juicy peaches, which he placed in his special travel pouch with his magic peach tree.

They all wished Gusto a safe journey as he effortlessly leapt into the air, his majestic body sailing gracefully towards the stars. Before he disappeared from view, he circled the sky above the Inside-Outside Garden, just as he had done on his arrival, blasting out the biggest gust of fire he had ever managed.

Everyone cheered in awe at the friendly dragon and they all agreed that this was the most exciting party they had ever been to.

Chapter 10
Sid Challenges Peaches

The next morning Peaches and Precious went down to the meadow to meet up with their friends. They all spent ages talking about the fun they had had at the party the previous evening.

Sid, the spider, who had been quieter than usual suddenly said, "Do you fancy a game of goal scoring Peaches?"

"You're a glutton for punishment Sid! How many points shall I give you to start with this time?" said Peaches, teasing him a little.

"I thought I might give *you* a few points to start with this morning, seeing as it was your birthday yesterday," replied Sid, forcing himself not to start laughing.

Sid could not resist teasing Peaches further. "Just to make it a bit more of a challenge, if you lose you have to clean all the mud off my eight legs and sweep all my old cobwebs away, but if you win then I have to do three forfeits of your choosing," said Sid confidently.

Peaches could not believe her ears. All the creatures in the meadow had heard Sid's challenge. They all started whistling, cheering and clapping. Peaches thought that Sid didn't stand a chance but somehow felt she had to take up his challenge or it would upset him, even though all their friends were now gathering around the goal area. The strange thing was, every time she looked at Sid, she just wanted to laugh. She had never seen him in such a serious, strange mood before.

The reason why Sid had never won any points was because, once he started laughing, he couldn't stop. He would normally laugh so much that Peaches would just keep scoring goals, knowing that he couldn't catch the ball because he was shaking so much with laughter. That is the reason why Peaches always won.

It was time for Sid to even the score! This time, he had his secret *strawberry wish* to help him!

As Sid walked between the goalposts, a wonderful feeling came over him. He began to feel like a superstar goalkeeper. He positioned himself between the posts looking determined, not taking his eyes off the ball. Peaches lined up her colourful ball and took six paces backwards. As she ran towards the ball she could feel Sid's eyes on her and the picture she had of him in her mind made her lose concentration. She

kicked the ball and it flew straight into Sid's
eight arms.

"Oh dear," said Sid, "better luck next time
Peaches!"

Peaches started to giggle as she attempted
her next goal and once again the ball went
directly into Sid's arms. It was as if the ball had a
mind of its own! The situation did not improve,
no matter how hard Peaches tried to kick the
ball into the net, it always seemed to find the
goalkeeper.

Sid had finally beaten Peaches! He was
triumphant!

With two of his black hairy legs held high
above his body, holding Peaches ball, he

paraded around the circle of meadow spectators. This was his moment of glory.

Peaches eventually picked herself up from the floor. She had laughed so much that her tummy ached. "Very funny Sid, congratulations!" said Peaches. "How on earth did you manage that? You must have been practising in your dreams!" She had no idea how Sid had won.

Peaches started to wash the mud off her friend's legs but it tickled Sid so much that she had to stop. The only thing left to do now was to sweep all his old cobwebs away, which Peaches did without hesitation. The meadow creatures looked on in admiration of the special friendship between Peaches and Sid. It was quite a sight seeing a fairy princess sweeping up old cobwebs!

Peaches reminded Sid that he had promised to arrange for all the fairies to play a proper game of football against his spider friends. He said that he would organise a special event later in the year, after Peaches and Precious had returned from their adventure in the Domain of the Dragons.

There were many adventures in store for Peaches and her friends.

Part 3

Gusto in the
Domain of the Dragons

Chapter 11
Journey to the Domain of the Dragons

Precious and Peaches went everywhere together but they were never happier than when they met up with Gusto the dragon, Peaches' special friend. They would all meet in the meadow at the foot of the Magic Mountains to play.

It was soon time for Peaches and Precious to prepare for their journey to the Domain of the Dragons, which lies beyond the Secret Islands of the Seven Clouds. Their dear friend Gusto, the giant dragon, was to compete in his first Dragon Games in the famous Dragon Arena. These games were only held every two hundred years.

The main event of the games was between the three strongest dragons. The prize was to become the Grand Protector of the Secret Islands of the Seven Clouds, which was the greatest honour to bestow on any dragon in the land.

Gusto had given Peaches and Precious an invitation to be his guests at this special occasion, as he had qualified to compete for this incredible honour. They were both getting very excited. Peaches had never before gone beyond her beloved meadow where she knew every blade of grass, and she was now to venture into unknown territory for the very first time.

Precious was exercising his 'magic' wings which, to people, were invisible but, Peaches could see them clearly. She was to nestle under his strong, downy feathers which would protect her whilst flying on the long journey to the Domain of the Dragons.

After careful planning, the day arrived when the two companions set off on their new adventure. They waved 'goodbye' to all their friends and family in the Kingdom of Wisdom. They were on their way.

It wasn't long before Peaches fell fast asleep in her cosy, warm bed beneath the protection of her pet's wings. She had many dreams, most of which involved Gusto whom she knew would be anxious at the forthcoming mammoth event. She comforted him in her dreams and sent whispers of encouragement and love, assuring him that he would be in her thoughts at all times. She also sent him unspoken messages of courage and support.

She woke up feeling wonderful and refreshed, the Domain of the Dragons was now in sight. Peaches was very excited!

As Precious approached, he could see Gusto waiting for them in front of the great, black, iron gates of the city. He looked amazing. He couldn't keep still in anticipation of seeing his two best friends.

Precious swooped down gently and landed in front of Gusto. He nearly landed on his back due to Gusto swaying from side to side

in sheer excitement at seeing his best friends again.

Peaches flew straight onto Gusto's knobbly dragon snout and gave him a big hug, her wings fluttering constantly, followed by Precious who licked the great dragon's head all over!

Gusto marched proudly through the great gates, with his friends on his huge upper jaw, showing them off to his fellow dragons, who nodded in awe and wonder at Gusto's friends. The dragons had never seen anyone enter their domain before, apart from other dragons.

Gusto was the envy of his dragon friends as, head held high, he paraded through the city to the banqueting hall, where he had prepared a welcome feast.

They were all hungry and enjoyed choosing from the platters of healthy food carefully prepared by their friend. Of course, the centre piece was a bowl of magnificent, fresh, juicy peaches, picked from Gusto's very own magic peach tree, given to him by Peaches at her birthday party. Every time he picked a peach, another one grew in its place. A bowl of peaches was always on the table for everyone to help themselves.

"You look so fit and healthy, Gusto!" said Peaches, with a big smile on her face, "I can tell you have been exercising and eating fruits and vegetables every day. *They have helped to keep nasty infections and diseases away, and helped to make you a fine example of a strong healthy dragon."*

Gusto's sister, Gradona, a rather shy, yet beautiful dragon, with long sweeping lashes and big bright eyes, showed Peaches and Precious to their sleeping quarters. Peaches' room was in the doll's house in the dragon nursery. Precious slept on a large woolly carpet in front of the doll's house. Here he could protect Peaches, although they both knew that they would not come to any harm.

The friends felt very safe and welcome, and both fell fast asleep into their own world of dreams. Tomorrow was the big day.

Chapter 12
The Big Day

The next morning, Peaches and Precious met with Gusto and his family for breakfast. Gusto had a dragon-sized bowl of porridge with lots of fresh raspberries and blueberries also, a spoonful of Manuka Honey sent especially for him from Peaches parents, King Manuka and Queen Honey.

Peaches knew that after breakfast they would have to part as Gusto had to go and prepare for his big ordeal. Before they parted Peaches had things she had to say to Gusto in private.

"Gusto," she said, do not be afraid today. You have the courage and ability to be the finest dragon in the history of The Dragon Games. Before going into the arena, calm yourself by taking three very long, slow, deliberate breaths then, breathe out, just as slowly. When the time comes to face your challenge in the grand arena, repeat this, then, take a fourth breath. On the fourth breath, inhale slowly as before but, give your outward breath as much gusto as you can muster, at the same time releasing your fire with every ounce of energy you have."

"Good luck Gusto! I know you will do your best! Precious and I will be supporting you every inch of the way," assured Peaches.

Gusto's whole family had special seats overlooking the main event in which Gusto was competing. Peaches and Precious sat on the front row between Gradona, Gusto's sister and Zola, Gusto's mother.

Peaches looked stunning. She wore a bright red silk blouse made from the finest silk in the Kingdom of Wisdom, a new pair of pale blue denim jeans, with a diamond studded belt and, of course, her favourite magic red trainers. Her jet black hair was tied in one long, thick plait down the back of her head, fastened with a red silk bow to match her pretty blouse.

Precious looked wonderful too. He had been bathed and groomed and was a ball of snow white fluff, apart from his two black eyes and big black nose. This was indeed a very special occasion.

The opening ceremony began with the dragon band marching all the way around the great arena. This was followed by a procession of all the dragons competing in the Grand Dragon Games. The last to join the parade were the three largest dragons, one of which was Gusto, who looked magnificent as he displayed his great stature and powerful muscles. These three dragons were to compete at the end of the games for the most prestigious prize of all; to be crowned, *"The Grand Protector of The Secret Islands of the Seven Clouds."*

After the excitement of all the other competitions, it was time for the most important challenge of all. The three giant dragons had to display their power by proving who could blow the longest fire from their nostrils.

In the first test, they had to blow their fire twenty-five metres towards the sky, to reach a fireproof pole, held in the air by two hovering dragons, one at each end.

The first dragon made his attempt and his fire flames easily licked the suspended pole held by the two dragon referees. The second dragon also managed to reach the target.

Peaches had noticed that Gusto was trembling slightly with nerves however, he also managed to reach the pole with his fire. The crowd applauded then fell into silence.

The pole was lifted to fifty metres above the arena. The first dragon took a deep breath and with great effort, blasted out a massive gust of fire which thinned out at its tail but still managed to reach the high pole. The second dragon also took a deep breath and, as he projected his fire, he gave out a strenuous noise, which shook the seats in which Precious and Peaches were sitting. Alas, his fire was just short of the pole. He was out of the competition. The vast audience applauded his effort then, once again, fell silent.

It was Gusto's turn. He could hear the silent whispers of Peaches echoing in his ears. "Take three slow, deep, breaths; think of nothing but the task in hand. Concentrate and believe in yourself. Take the fourth breath slowly, then, release all your breath and energy in a whirl of hot fire."

Gusto calmed himself and followed the silent advice of his fairy friend and with a blast of effort, easily managed to reach the pole with his volcanic fire. His remaining opponent looked on in amazement. The crowd loved it. They had a real competition to witness and the suspense was electric!

The pole was raised yet again, to an incredible one hundred metres but this time, the pole was made of *wood*. Could either dragon manage this superdragon task? The only dragon to have ever have reached this great length of fire was Samson, the first Protector of the Secret Islands of the Seven Clouds, many hundreds of years ago.

Peaches and Precious had both noticed the anger in the eyes of the opposing giant as he took his position for the final challenge. He was astonished when Gusto achieved his last challenge; he had expected to have won by now. This was indeed a tense moment.

As he blew the fire from his bursting nostrils, his big red eyes nearly popped out of his head, and the exertion made the veins on his neck stand out like tree branches spreading down his great chest. In spite of his mammoth effort, the fire was short of the pole by about twenty metres. Hc retreated exhausted and panting for breath.

As Gusto walked forward to take up his position, his exhausted opponent managed to stamp the ground in anger, in an effort to put Gusto off, making the ground tremble beneath Gusto's feet and disturbing his concentration for his final attempt at reaching the pole. Precious, watching what was happening, twitched his magic nose. Almost immediately the dragon stopped his tantrum and sat peacefully at the side of the arena as Gusto continued to prepare for the challenge of his life.

You could hear a pin drop. Even the birds had stopped singing, as they held their delicate breath. Was history to be made before their very eyes, or would there have to be a play off for the winner of this unbelievable competition?

Gusto closed his eyes to concentrate. Once again he thought of the warm breath of Peaches, whispering advice. He took three very deep, long, slow breaths, all the time thinking of Peaches and the power their friendship had given him. He was suddenly in his own world, unaware of the spectacular scene surrounding him. Gusto drew his fourth breath deeper into his soul than ever before, his eyes opened in total concentration, as his head lifted slowly heaven-wards towards the pole.

He expelled his breath with every ounce of energy his body possessed.

The unbelievable breath of fire stretched out, embracing the wooden pole in the sky. It burned instantly into ashes under the intense heat of Gusto's volcanic fire and fell down into the crowd as tiny pieces of twinkling stardust.

Chapter 13
The Grand Protector

The crowd rose to their feet in disbelief and ecstatic joy as they cheered their champion dragon. Gusto was lifted into the air by his two competitors who carried him around the arena. The crowd were overjoyed, shouting a chorus of, "GUSTO! GUSTO! GUSTO!" He was their hero.

Gusto was presented with the red and gold band of honour, only worn by *The Grand Protector of The Secret Islands of the Seven Clouds*, to the great roar of the spectators. He wore it with great pride around his massive neck.

The crowd was still cheering, as Gusto beckoned Peaches and Precious to join him. He gave his final lap of honour, with Peaches on his warm snout and Precious on top of his head. The three of them soaked up the adoration of the crowd, before making their exit from the famous dragon arena.

A new era had begun. What Gusto didn't realise, was that his life would soon change forever. Within a few months he would embark on a journey of discovery and adventure which would ultimately lead him to his destiny.

Precious handed Gusto the biggest and most juicy peach he had ever seen. It just appeared out of thin air! "Ooh, where did this come from?" cried Gusto. "Someone must have

read my mind! It's just what I need right now."

Precious winked at Peaches! He had used his

magic to produce the giant peach, to refresh the

new champion.

"We knew you could do it, Gusto.

Congratulations! We are so proud of you," said

Peaches.

"I couldn't have done it without you,

Peaches. You made me believe in myself and

you taught me how to eat healthy foods, instead

of all that junk food I used to eat. How can I

ever repay you?" said Gusto.

"That's what friends are for and besides,

we have just had the most fantastic time. We

wouldn't have missed this for anything," said

Peaches. Precious nodded in agreement, whilst

licking Gusto's head, partly in affection and partly to cool him down from his hot ordeal.

"We both feel very privileged to have such a famous and powerful friend," remarked Peaches proudly. Gusto relished this moment of adoration from his two friends.

"Race you to the lagoon for a dip!" said Gusto.

They all splashed about laughing and having fun before going home to reflect on the most magical of days.

Chapter 14

Gusto Visits the
Dragon Children's Training Camp

A few days had passed since Gusto became The
Grand Protector of the Secret Islands of the
Seven Clouds at the famous Dragon Games,
when Gusto was asked to visit the Dragon
Children's Fitness Camp, to help dragon children
become fit and healthy. The trainers believed
that Gusto might be able to inspire the children,
as they had not stopped talking about him since
he won the red and gold band of honour. He
was their hero.

Gusto, Peaches and Precious had a meeting to discuss their plan of action and couldn't wait to meet the dragon children.

Gusto took a large bag of fruit. Precious took a bag full of fresh vegetables and Peaches made a large berry crumble, which Gusto carried because it was very heavy. It was a special treat for those children who followed their trainer's advice.

As they approached the fitness camp they noticed that the windows had big dragon noses squeezed up against them They belonged to several dragon children waiting to get a good view of their hero!

Mr. Slimsnout, the head trainer, met the three friends and introduced them to ten young dragons, five girls and five boys, who were sitting in a semi-circle in the centre of the meeting room.

The young dragons had been making lots of noise in their excitement at meeting Gusto but, as soon as he walked into the room, they all fell silent. The silence lasted about three seconds, then one of the boys cried, "Three cheers for The Grand Protector". Precious could have sworn that the whole building shook with all the loud cheering!

"Well, thankyou so much for that fantastic welcome. I certainly didn't expect so much enthusiasm! I hope you all think as much of me when I leave, as you do now," said Gusto, wondering how they would receive his carefully worked out plan.

"I would like to introduce you to my friends, Princess Peaches from the Kingdom of Wisdom in the Magic Mountains, and Precious, Peaches guardian. I will begin by telling you how we met," said Gusto, as the dragon children listened intently to his every word.

Gusto then explained to the children how he had once been a very unfit dragon, with no energy and that he couldn't even blow a single flame of fire from his nostrils. When the children heard this, they couldn't believe their ears and a gasp of disbelief swept through the room. He continued the story up to where he first met Peaches; how she had appeared, as if from nowhere, at the edge of his pool of tears in Bluebell Wood under the old oak tree.

"Peaches, would you please tell the rest of the story to the children," asked Gusto politely.

"It would be my pleasure," replied Peaches, delighted that Gusto had given her this opportunity to prove a very important point to the children.

Peaches slowly and deliberately commenced with the story. "When I met Gusto he was very, very sad. Apart from only being able to blow a puff of smoke from his giant nostrils, he felt wretched and tired all the time."

"I soon discovered that Gusto had been eating lots of unhealthy foods and not taking any exercise. I told him that if he wanted to become a fit and healthy dragon again, he would have to start eating plenty of fresh fruit and vegetables every day. I told him that I would help him by proving how delicious healthy food is."

"Gusto was very good. He really enjoyed the healthy foods I gave him and just look at him now! You could all be fit and healthy, just like Gusto, if you start eating fresh fruit and vegetables every day," said Peaches.

The children were all listening hard to the story of their new hero and how he met his friend. Peaches and Gusto had their full attention. Gusto continued, "We have brought you some delicious, fresh, healthy fruits and vegetables to try."

Precious then gave everyone a juicy peach, including Gusto, Peaches and himself.

When the dragon children saw Gusto enjoying his peach so much they all started to bite into theirs. They had all eaten the peach within seconds, the stone as well! They had never tasted a peach before.

"Would you like an apple now?" asked Precious, dipping into his large bag of fresh fruit."

The children all yelled, "Yes please!" Ten minutes later, the bag of fruit had disappeared into the bellies of the dragon children.

"We have given the dinner ladies a large bag of fresh vegetables to cook for your next meal," said Gusto, to looks of disapproval on the faces of the children. "Don't worry, there is roast chicken and potatoes as well! We will all be having dinner together and, if you don't eat any unhealthy food for the rest of the day, you can have some of Peaches' super Berry Crumble. She has made this especially for those of you who stick to the fitness camp rules. In the meantime, who wants to come with us for a walk in the country?"

Needless to say, they all volunteered to join their hero; they were delighted to be going for a walk with Gusto and his friends. As they set off across the fields, the last thing on their minds was eating. They chatted and laughed, and listened to many stories about Gusto and his favourite playmates as they trundled through the beautiful countryside.

After a long walk up hill and down dale, the dragons returned to the fitness camp. They all had warm showers and then joined the three friends in the dining room. The smell was fantastic and they were hungry! The only thing they had eaten since lunch time was fresh fruit.

Everything was eaten, even the carrots, broccoli and spinach and guess what - they enjoyed every mouthful!

"Are you forgetting something?" said one of the young girl dragons, in a gentle voice. Before Gusto could reply, one of the dinner ladies brought out the huge berry crumble that Peaches had made, with a large jug of custard. "You can get stuck in!" said Gusto. "You have all well-deserved this special treat. *It's made with lots of berries, which have magic powers to help fight nasty infections and diseases.* We have given the recipe to the dinner ladies so that you may have a portion of berry crumble every evening, providing you eat regular healthy meals, take daily exercise and eat fresh fruit for snacks."

"I'm going to be checking up on each one of you to see how you progress," said Gusto. "I will arrange a game of rounders before my friends leave in two days time. Only those of you who stick to fitness camp rules will be able to join us."

"We'll be there Gusto!" shouted the young dragons. They were not going to miss an opportunity to play rounders with their hero.

Gusto visited the dragon children often and every week he saw a remarkable difference in their health and fitness. They soon became so fit and healthy that they left the fitness camp.

The young determined dragons returned home and formed a Rounders Club for all the young dragons in The Domain of the Dragons. Gusto was their mascot and they encouraged all the other dragons to eat fruit and vegetables every day.

PEACHES FAVOURITE HEALTHY BERRY CRUMBLE

Serves 6

Peaches likes this Berry Crumble because it contains
lots of berries which *help to fight nasty infections and diseases.*

Crumble mix

Approx 675g Frozen Berries
2/3 Heaped desert spoons runny honey
Ovenproof dish large enough to hold berries with
the crumble topping

In a separate bowl mix:

110g Wholemeal Flour
50g Ground Almonds
75g Good Quality Margarine
1 Desert Spoon Raw Cane Granulated Sugar
Handful Flaked Almonds to sprinkle on top

To make

First, place the berries in the oven proof dish and drizzle over honey.
Next make the crumble: Put the wholemeal flower, ground almonds and
margarine into a separate bowl and gently rub them together to make the
crumble. It should look like breadcrumbs. Then stir the sugar into the
crumble mixture. Spread the crumble evenly over the top of the berries.
Sprinkle the flaked almonds on top.
Bake for approx 30 minutes.
Electric 180° C. Gas mark 5/375°F.

Serve with yogurt, custard or single cream.

MESSAGE FOR MUMS

Because this crumble contains nuts, it is not advisable to give to under five year olds or pregnant women. You can, however, substitute the ground almonds for wholemeal flour or rolled oats and omit the flaked almonds.

If your children are over five years old and do not have a nut allergy, this crumble is very nutritious. It is extremely quick and easy to make.

Fruits and vegetables are full of many potent anti-oxidants which are essential for building a strong immune system. Berries in particular are rich in anti-oxidants.

You can read more about Gusto's

adventures in . . .

. . . Book 2

The Secret Islands of the Seven Clouds